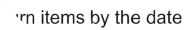
rn items by the date

Steve
Smallman

Migy
Blanco

BAD
BUNNY!

SCHOLASTIC

Who likes breaking **every** rule?

Who made Tortoise look a **fool**?

Who did a piddle
in the paddling pool...?

BAD BUNNY!

To look at him you'd think that he

was just as sweet as he could be,

but turn your back
and soon you'll see...

Who looks up with big wide eyes
when he's telling great big lies?

Who's been eating
all the pies?

BURP!

BAD BUNNY!

Who made Grandma's face go red,
running through the flower bed,
wearing knickers on his head?

BAD BUNNY!

His mummy said, "Oh, Bunny Boo,
if you play tricks the way you do,
one day the trick will be on you!"

He didn't listen.

Who put glue in Badger's socks?

Who cut holes in the cereal box?

Who got...

...caught by

Who is feeling very hot?

Who would really rather not

be in Fox's cooking pot?

BAD BUNNY!

Who has got no friends to call?

Who played tricks upon them all?

Who is feeling very small?

BAD BUNNY!

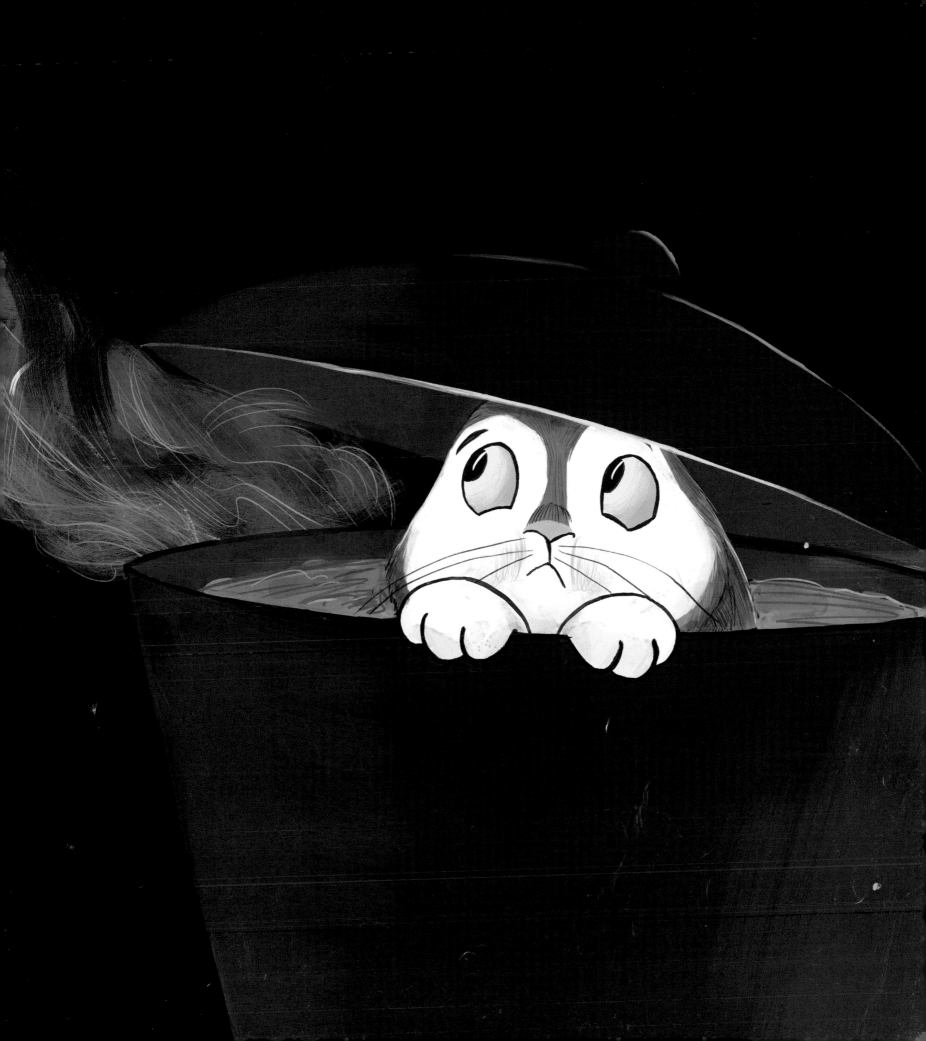

"Dear Fox" he cried,

"I'm begging you please don't eat this rabbit stew

because it's full of..."

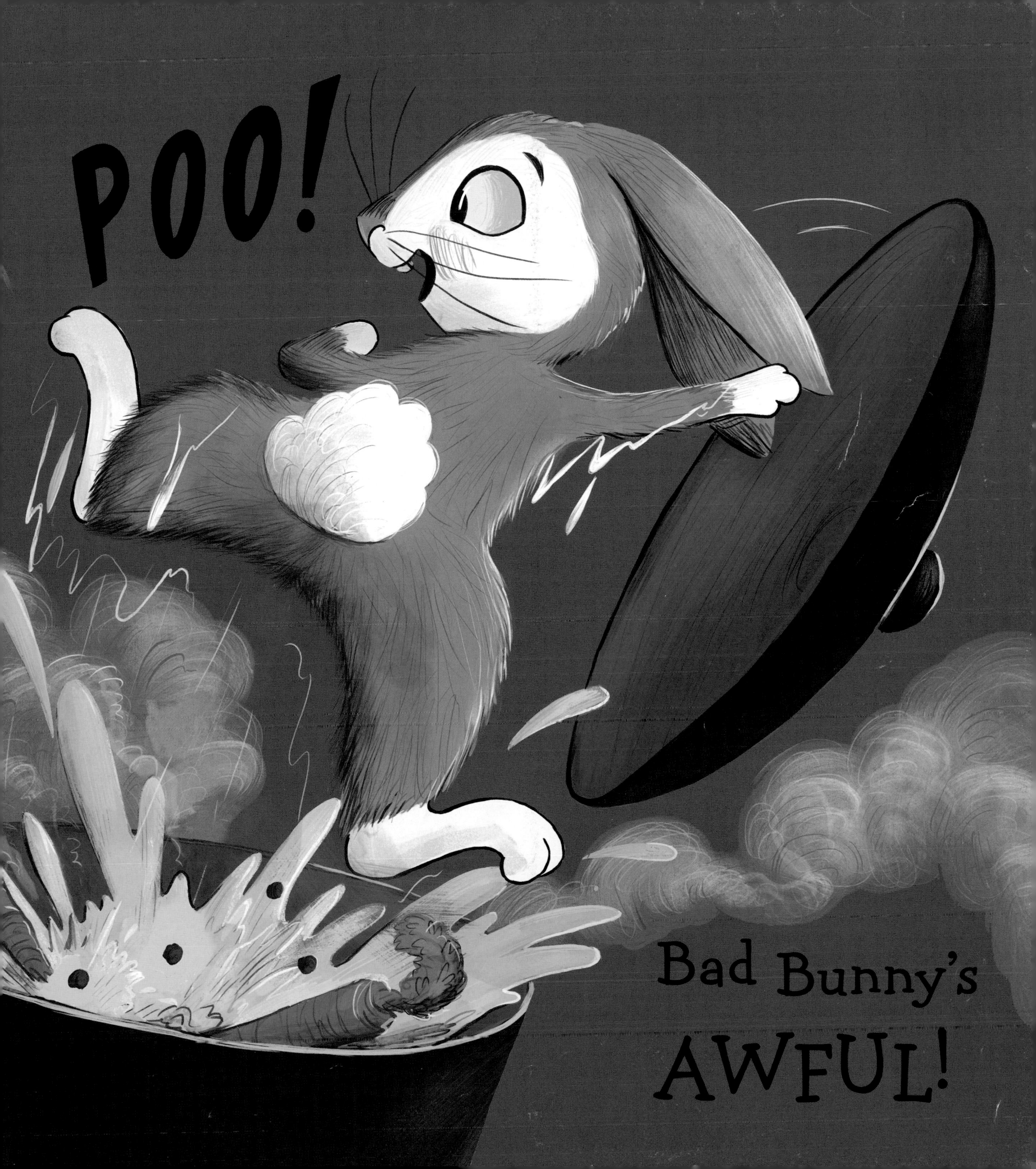
POO!
Bad Bunny's
AWFUL!

Who is running down the path?

Who shouts,

"Thank you for the bath!"

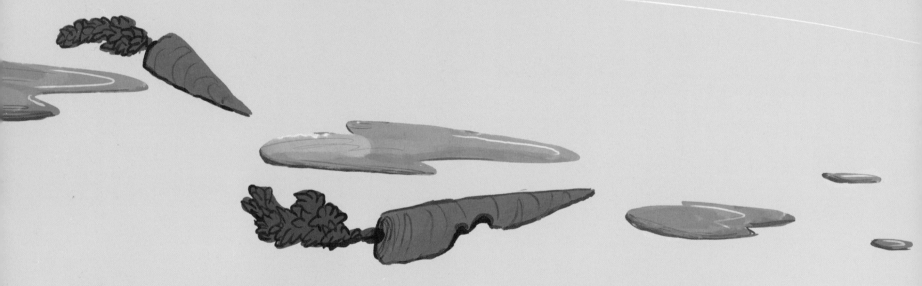

Who is having such a laugh?

BAD

BUNNY!

For Avery, who also likes breaking every rule!
S.S.

For the cheeky little chap Benicio
M.B.

First published in 2018 by Scholastic Children's Books
Euston House, 24 Eversholt Street
London NW1 1DB
a division of Scholastic Ltd
www.scholastic.co.uk
London ~ New York ~ Toronto ~ Sydney ~ Auckland
Mexico City ~ New Delhi ~ Hong Kong

Text copyright © 2018 Steve Smallman
Illustrations copyright © 2018 Migy Blanco

PB ISBN 978 1407 18168 4